I0747228

THE FLOW OF ZEN

21 Short Stories on Being Present, Letting Go of Anxiety, and Living with Ease

The Zen Storyteller
Book 2

KAI TSUKIMI

Dedicated to Kat

© Copyright 2025 Kai Tsukimi – Omen Publishing LLC - All rights reserved.

The content of this book may not be reproduced, duplicated, or transmitted without direct written permission from the author or the publisher.

Under no circumstances will any blame or legal responsibility be held against the publisher or author for any damages, reparation, or monetary loss due to use of the information contained within this book, either directly or indirectly.

Legal Notice:

This book is copyright protected. It is for personal use only. You cannot amend, distribute, sell, use, quote, or paraphrase any part, or the content within this book, without the consent of the author or publisher.

Disclaimer Notice:

Please note the information contained within this document is for educational and entertainment purposes only. All effort has been executed to present accurate, up-to-date, reliable, complete information. No warranties of any kind are declared or implied. Readers acknowledge the author is not engaging in the rendering of legal, financial, medical, or professional advice. The information is this book has been gleaned from various sources as well as from the author's own creativity.

A book can shift your perspective, but a ritual can transform your life. As a thank-you for reading, I'd like to offer you our exclusive *Zen Clarity Kit*, designed to help you clear your mind, refocus, and make Zen teachings a part of your daily routine.

What's Inside the Kit?

✓ **The Zen Morning Ritual Guide** – A simple daily practice to anchor your mind in stillness.

✓ **A 5-Minute Audio Meditation** – Gently guide yourself into a state of clarity and focus.

✓ **Zen Minimalism Wallpapers** – Subtle reminders to cultivate presence throughout your day.

>> Scan the QR Code or click here to download your free gift <<

Table of Contents

Introduction

What Is Flow?

To understand flow, imagine a river. It moves effortlessly, winding through valleys, bending around stones, and always following the path of least resistance. Instead of fighting the obstacles in its path, it flows around them. It does not cling to the past or chase after the future. It just moves.

Now, imagine that river is your life. But instead of flowing, you resist. You grip tightly to control, to certainty, to how you think things *should* be. You struggle against the current, exhausting yourself in the process.

This is where Zen comes in.

Zen isn't about forcing life to go your way. It's about *moving with life*, just as water moves with the shape of the land. It's about learning when to act and when to let go. It's about finding peace, not by holding on, but by surrendering to the natural rhythm of things.

Most of us spend our days grasping—chasing after what we want, pushing away what we fear. But Zen teaches us a different way: the way of flow. And one of the best ways to understand flow? Stories.

What Are Zen Stories?

Think about the last time something unexpected shifted your perspective—a simple moment that made you see things differently. Maybe it was a conversation, a piece of art, or the way sunlight moved across a wall. Some truths don't arrive through explanations. They arrive through experience.

Zen stories are like that. They don't *tell* you what to think. They invite you to *see* something for yourself. Sometimes the story is subtle.

Strange. Mystical. Sometimes the story makes no sense at all—until, suddenly, it does.

A Zen master once said, "Let go, or be dragged." Meaning? Life will keep moving, whether you cling or not. Zen stories help loosen your grip. They remind you that not everything needs an answer, not everything needs control. Sometimes, the wisest thing you can do is allow things to be as they are.

This book is a collection of 21 Zen stories, each one designed to help you see the peace in letting go, moving with life, and trusting in the natural flow of things.

How Do I Use This Book?

First rule: There are no rules.

Read this book however you want. Open it randomly, read one story a day, or finish it in one sitting. There's no right way to experience Zen.

But if you'd like a suggestion—try reading one story a day for 21 days. Let it sit with you. Don't rush to figure it out. Just let it flow through your mind like water over stones.

Some stories will be clear. Others might leave you wondering. That's the point.

After each story, you'll find a simple reflection—a thought, a question, or a small practice to try in your own life. There's nothing to force. Just let the ideas settle like ripples fading on a still pond.

Because the truth is, you don't have to *grasp* Zen—you just have to stop resisting what is already here.

And that starts by going with the flow.

— Kai

PART I
Awakening To Presence

Drink your tea slowly and reverently, as if it is the axis on which the world revolves.

Thich Nhat Hanh

1

———

THE WHISPERING STONE

A YOUNG MONK NAMED KISHO wandered the monastery grounds, troubled by a question that refused to leave him: "What does it mean to truly listen?" His master, old and silent as a mountain, had given no answer, only a small smile that deepened the riddle in Kisho's heart.

One morning, while sweeping fallen leaves near the temple's entrance, Kisho struck something solid beneath the soil. He bent over and brushed the dirt away, revealing a smooth, round stone. It was unremarkable—gray, cool to the touch, as ordinary as any other stone in the temple garden.

Yet, something about it held Kisho's attention. He grabbed it and held it in the palm of his hand. Then, remembering his question, he closed his eyes and listened.

At first, there was only silence.

Then, the wind passed through the trees, rustling the branches. Birds called to one another in the distance. The faint murmur of monks chanting from within the hall wove through the morning air. And still, he listened. He heard the whisper of his own breath, the steady rhythm of his heart, the quiet hum of existence itself.

And within all of it—the stone remained.

Kisho exhaled slowly and opened his eyes, suddenly understanding. He carried the stone to his master and placed it before him. The master, seeing it, nodded.

"You have heard well," he said at last.

Kisho bowed, no longer needing any further words.

Reflection

When was the last time you listened—not just with your ears, but with your whole being?
What did you discover?

The stone neither spoke nor moved, yet it revealed something profound.
What in your life might be quietly teaching you, if only you paused to listen?

———

A Moment of Zen

Sit with an object in silence.
Observe it without judgment.

Close your eyes and listen to the farthest and closest sounds.

Move through your day like the stone—
present, steady, at ease.

2

THE SOUP THAT STIRRED ITSELF

THE KITCHEN OF MASTER REN'S
teahouse was always filled with steam, the scent

of simmering broth, and the rhythmic chop of a knife against wood. A young apprentice, Jiro, had been assigned the humbling task of stirring the soup. He stood by the great iron pot, wooden spoon in hand, watching the broth swirl beneath his touch.

The day was ending. As the sun cast amber light through the paper windows, Jiro's patience faltered. He approached Master Ren, frustration simmering like the soup. "Why must I stir this endlessly? The broth moves, yet nothing changes."

Master Ren did not reply. Instead, he led Jiro outside to the garden pond. The surface was still, reflecting the sky like a perfect mirror. Master Ren bent down, dipped a finger into the water, and traced a slow circle. Ripples spread outward, distorting the reflection before fading into stillness.

Jiro watched, puzzled. "But the pond moves only when disturbed."

Master Ren turned back toward the teahouse. "Perhaps, then, the soup is not waiting for you to stir it."

That night, as Jiro returned to the pot, he hesitated before touching the spoon. The steam curled upward, the broth shimmered. He stood still, only watching. And in the depths of the pot, something shifted. The soup, left alone, continued to turn.

Reflection

Where in your life do you stir too much, mistaking motion for progress?

What happens when you allow things to unfold without interference?

———

A Moment of Zen

Pour a cup of tea and watch the steam rise.
Do nothing but observe.

Place a bowl of water before you.
Dip a finger in, then wait for stillness.

The next time you feel restless, pause.
Let the moment settle on its own.

3

THE BAMBOO BRIDGE

How do you trust what shifts beneath you?

Sora stood at the edge of the bamboo bridge, watching it sway over the wide river. The rain had passed, but the current still churned violently below.

An old ferryman, watching from his hut, stepped out as Sora hesitated at the edge. "It looks unsteady," Sora said. "Will it hold?"

The ferryman smiled but gave no answer. He picked up a fallen leaf and dropped it onto the bridge. The leaf trembled, then settled.

Sora frowned. "A leaf is not a man."

The ferryman gestured toward the river. "Is the water solid?"

"Of course not," Sora replied. "It is always moving."

"And yet, does it not hold the boats?" the ferryman asked, before stepping back into his hut.

Sora looked at the bridge again. The wind sighed through the bamboo, the river rushed below, the leaf lay still.

Taking a breath, he placed one foot forward.

Reflection

What structures in your life feel unsteady, yet may be stronger than you assume?

How do you determine whether to trust the ground beneath you?

A Moment of Zen

Stand barefoot on the earth.
Feel how it supports you, even as it shifts.

Watch a floating leaf.
Observe its movement and stillness.

Cross a bridge slowly.
With each step, notice trust and hesitation.

4

THE LANTERN AND THE MOTH

THE MOTH STRUCK THE LANTERN OVER

and over, its wings tapping softly against the warm glass.

After abandoning his meditation, Daichi watched. He was drawn instead to the creature's restless dance. Again and again, it approached, drawn by the light, only to retreat at the last moment.

Why did the moth hesitate? Why did it not surrender to the flame or turn away completely?

The temple's old abbot, unseen until now, spoke softly from the shadows. "Why do you sit in meditation, Daichi?"

Daichi hesitated, then replied, "To find clarity."

The abbot nodded toward the moth. "And yet, you watch."

Daichi turned back to the lantern. The moth still circled, neither embracing nor abandoning the flame. He closed his eyes, listening to the soft hum of its wings, feeling the warmth of the lantern on his skin.

When he opened them again, the moth had disappeared into the darkness.

Reflection

What is the flame you are drawn to, yet fear to touch?

How do you know when to approach and when to step away?

———

A Moment of Zen

Light a candle and sit with it.
Observe the pull of its glow.

Watch an insect's movement—
its hesitation, its certainty.

Sit in stillness.
Notice what draws your attention, then let
it go.

5

A FEATHER ON THE WIND

THE MARKET SQUARE HUMMED WITH motion—merchants shouting, carts rattling, footsteps weaving through the dust. Kaito moved quickly, a sealed letter pressed against his chest. The governor was waiting. There was no time to waste.

A gust of wind spiraled through the alley, lifting a white feather into the air. It wove between stalls, rose, dipped, then settled on Kaito's path. His boot paused mid-step.

An old vendor, stacking oranges, chuckled. "Chasing it won't help."

Kaito frowned. "I wasn't chasing it."

The vendor only smiled, tossing an orange from one hand to the other, waiting. Kaito kept moving—but his pace had slowed. The feather lifted again, swirling away, indifferent to urgency.

The scent of roasted chestnuts drifted past. A flute played somewhere beyond the square. Kaito loosened his grip on the letter. The letter still needed to be delivered. But now, he wondered if it truly had to be this very moment.

He stood still, just for a breath, and watched the feather disappear into the sky.

Reflection

When was the last time something small made you pause?
What did it reveal?

What are you rushing toward, and what might happen if you slowed down?

———

A Moment of Zen

Stand in a busy place and close your eyes for a moment. Feel the movement around you.

Let an unexpected delay unfold without resistance. Notice what arises.

Watch something carried by the wind—a leaf, dust, or feather. Follow it without moving.

PART II
The Dance of Effortless Action

Do you have the patience to wait until
your mud settles and the water is clear?

Lao Tzu

6

———

THE RIVER THAT REFUSED TO FLOW

THE RIVER HAD STOPPED MOVING. Haku stood at its edge, as the water pooled unnaturally still while the current rushed past on either side.

This river was famous amongst travelers. They often stood by the riverbank to whisper their worries to the water, watching their reflections ripple and fade.

One day, a young monk named Haku arrived at the river's edge, seeking solace from his restless thoughts. He cupped his hands in the water and let the cool stream slip through his fingers. Yet as he gazed at the current, something strange caught his eye—a section of the river ahead was motionless.

Puzzled, Haku went to investigate. The water did not move. It pooled, clear and still, while the rest of the river continued to flow. He dipped his hand in; the surface barely trembled. It was as though this part of the river had decided to stop.

An old fisherman, sitting nearby, watched him with quiet amusement.

"This river refuses to flow," Haku said, turning to him. "How can this be?"

The fisherman cast his line into the water, letting it rest. "Perhaps it does not refuse," he said. "Perhaps it is waiting."

Haku frowned. "A river must move. That is its nature."

The fisherman said nothing. He simply pointed downstream. Haku followed the gesture and saw how, just beyond the stillness, the water surged forward again, faster than before, tumbling over rocks in a white froth before smoothing out once more.

Haku stood in silence. The river had not stopped; it had only gathered itself. He looked back at the fisherman, but the old man had already reeled in his empty line and was walking away.

Haku sat on the bank, listening. The river, patient and unhurried, carried on.

Reflection

When have you mistaken stillness for stagnation?

In what moments have you needed to pause before moving forward?

———

A Moment of Zen

Find a stream or fountain.
Observe how it moves, where it slows, where it rushes.

Sit in stillness for a few moments.
Notice the urge to act, then let it pass.

The next time you feel stuck, imagine yourself as the river—pausing, but never truly stopped.

7

THE ARCHER AND THE ARROW

IN THE MOUNTAINS BEYOND THE
temple, a master archer named Kai practiced in

solitude. His arrows cut through the mist, striking the wooden target with unwavering precision. Each shot was perfect.

A wandering monk approached, drawn by the rhythmic sound of the arrows finding their mark. He watched in silence for a while before speaking.

"Your aim is flawless, but is it effortless?"

Kai frowned. "What do you mean? I have trained for years to perfect my shot."

The monk picked up a fallen twig and tossed it into the air. The wind caught it, sending it tumbling through the sky before it landed softly on the earth. "The twig has no effort, yet it follows its path."

Kai scoffed. "A twig is not an arrow. An arrow must be guided."

The monk smiled. "Then shoot without guiding."

Curious, Kai pulled out another arrow and lifted his bow. He aimed, exhaled, and let the arrow fly—but at the last moment, his fingers twitched to correct the shot. The arrow veered slightly, missing the center.

The monk simply bowed and walked away.

That night, as the wind sighed through the trees, Kai sat with his bow across his lap. The twig had flown without resistance. His arrow had not. He watched the stars and wondered which path was truly straight.

Reflection

**When have you overcorrected something
that may have been fine on its own?**

**How do you distinguish between control
and trust in your own actions?**

———

A Moment of Zen

Toss a small object into the air.
Observe how it moves without effort.

Try completing a familiar task without
overthinking. Notice how it feels.

Stand in the wind.
Let it move you before you decide to move
yourself.

8

THE CLOUD'S JOURNEY

HIGH IN THE HILLS, WHERE THE WIND
carried the scent of pine and the river carved its

song into the valley below, a young monk named Sogen watched the clouds drift across the sky. He had spent years in the monastery, yet his mind remained restless, anxious, and filled with thoughts of the future.

As the sun set, the old abbot found Sogen sitting alone, eyes fixed on the heavens.

"Tell me, Sogen," the abbot said, lowering himself onto a nearby rock. "Where do the clouds go?"

Sogen frowned. "They travel where the wind takes them."

The abbot nodded. "And do they resist?"

Sogen shook his head. "No, they simply move."

The abbot picked up a dry leaf and released it to the breeze. It tumbled and spun before settling gently on the ground. "And this leaf?"

"The wind carries it too," Sogen replied.

"And the river?" the abbot said, as he pointed down to the valley.

Sogen did not answer.

The abbot turned his gaze toward the horizon. "Why do you resist?"

Sogen wanted to answer, but did not know how. He watched as a lone cloud stretched and dissolved into the endless blue sky, its journey complete.

That evening, Sogen packed his few belongings and started to walk. He did not know where he would go, only that the wind had already begun to carry him.

Reflection

In what ways do you resist the natural flow of life?

What would it mean for you to move like the clouds, without resistance?

———

A Moment of Zen

Watch the sky for a few minutes.
Observe how the clouds shift without effort.

Hold a leaf in your hand, then let it go.
Follow its path without interfering.

The next time you feel uncertain, take one step forward without overthinking.

9

———

THE MASTER WHO NEVER MOVED

THERE WAS ONCE A RENOWNED
swordsman named Renshu who lived at the

edge of a quiet village. Despite the isolation, his reputation spread far beyond the valley. It was said that no one had ever seen him draw his sword, and yet, he never faced defeat.

One day, a young warrior named Daiki arrived in the village, eager to challenge the master. He had spent years perfecting his technique, defeating opponents in countless duels. Certain that his speed and precision would surpass any man, he made his way to Renshu's small wooden house.

Standing before the old master, Daiki bowed. "I have come to challenge you."

Renshu, sitting cross-legged on his porch, did not look up. "Then strike."

Daiki hesitated. The old man's stillness unsettled him. He drew his sword in a single motion, the blade gleaming in the afternoon light. But before he could step forward, something held him back. The master had not moved, had not reacted, or even blinked.

The wind shifted. A leaf spiraled to the ground. Daiki's grip tightened, yet still, the master remained as he was—silent, unmoving, present.

Moments passed. The tension in Daiki's body began to fade. The energy he had built up, the intent to strike, all drained away like water slipping through open fingers. His arms fell to his side. He took a step back, then another, then bowed deeply.

Renshu finally looked up and smiled.

Daiki sheathed his sword and left the village without a duel, yet knowing he had already lost.

Reflection

What does it mean to win without fighting?

How does stillness challenge the need for action?

———

A Moment of Zen

Sit in a chair and resist the urge to adjust your posture. Notice what arises.

Observe someone engaged in an argument. Without taking sides, feel the energy between words.

Place an object in front of you. Look at it deeply without labeling or defining it.

10

THE GATE THAT WAS NEVER CLOSED

For years, Jun sought the wisdom of Master Tenzin, a hermit who lived atop a mountain shrouded in mist. The villagers spoke of his deep insight, yet no one had seen him take a student. Despite being aware of this, Jun climbed the steep path, determined to prove his worth.

Reaching the summit, he found a wooden gate marking the entrance to the master's home. It stood slightly ajar. Jun hesitated, then proceeded to knock. No answer came. He knocked again. More silence. He waited, shifting from foot to foot, before finally pushing the gate open.

Inside, he found a simple garden, a teapot steaming over a small fire, and Master Tenzin seated nearby, sipping his tea.

Jun bowed deeply. "Master, I have come a great distance to learn from you."

Tenzin took another sip and nodded toward the gate. "Did anyone stop you from entering?"

Jun blinked. "No, Master."

"Then why did you knock?"

Jun did not know. He looked back at the gate, then down at his own hands. A realization dawned on him. The path had never been blocked; only his hesitation had kept him outside.

Tenzin poured another cup of tea and gestured for Jun to sit.

Reflection

What doors in your life have been open all along, though you hesitated to walk through them?

How often do you wait for permission when none is needed?

———

A Moment of Zen

The next time you approach a door, pause. Notice your instinct before entering.

Sit with a warm cup of tea. Feel the heat, the weight, the presence of the moment.

Reflect on an opportunity you delayed acting on.
What held you back?

PART III

The Art of Seeing

Each moment is a place you've never been.

Mark Strand

11

THE LAST BLOSSOM

WHY HAD THE TREE NOT BLOOMED?

A young monk named Jiraya sat beneath its bare branches, tracing fallen petals from seasons past into the dirt.

Many other monks in the area would whisper among themselves. Some said the tree had grown too old. Others believed it had simply chosen silence. Yet, hidden among its weathered branches, a single bud remained—small, delicate, and unnoticed.

Jiraya often sat beneath the tree, gazing at its branches. He had spent months struggling with doubt, questioning his practice, his path, and the meaning of his devotion. One evening, weary from his thoughts, he looked up and saw it; *the lone bud trembling against the sky.*

Jiraya rose and approached the tree. He reached out but did not touch it, watching instead as the bud shivered in the breeze. He sat back down and waited.

Days passed. The other monks carried on, no longer speaking of the silent tree. Yet Jiraya returned every morning, watching the bud swell ever so slightly, its petals still curled tightly against the cold.

One morning, just as the first rays of sunlight touched the mountain peaks, Jiraya found himself by the tree once more. There, in the hush of dawn, the single blossom had opened. Pale pink, fragile, yet whole. Jiraya felt something shift within him. He exhaled and bowed deeply.

When he turned to leave, he did not look back.

Reflection

What in your life is quietly waiting to bloom?

How do you respond when things do not unfold in the time you expect?

A Moment of Zen

Observe a plant, tree, or flower for a few minutes. Notice its stillness and quiet growth.

Hold something delicate in your hand. Pay attention to its texture, weight, and presence.

The next time you find yourself impatient, pause.
Let the moment unfold in its own time.

12

THE LANTERN THAT FADED

THE LANTERN BURNED TOO FAST. A young monk named Minato watched as the oil in its base drained lower, the flame flickering strongly as if it knew its own fate. He had placed it there, ensuring it would last through the night.

As the hours passed, the temple quieted. The other monks had retreated to their quarters, their lanterns steady and subdued. Yet Minato's lantern continued to burn with an almost restless energy, its flame consuming the oil faster than expected. Minato, unable to sleep, watched from the corridor, his gaze fixed on the trembling light.

An elderly monk, Fumiko, walked down the hall and sat beside him. "You seem troubled," she said softly.

Minato hesitated before replying. "This lantern burns too fiercely. It may not last until morning."

Fumiko nodded, her eyes reflecting the wavering light. "And yet, does it not fulfill its purpose?"

Minato frowned. "But it wastes itself too quickly. At least the others will last the night."

Fumiko smiled and gestured toward the temple garden, where the petals of a late-blooming flower trembled in the breeze. "Would you call a flower's brief bloom wasted?"

Minato looked back at the lantern just as the last of its oil vanished. With one final flicker, the flame surrendered to the night. The room dimmed, yet the silence it left behind felt fuller somehow, as if the light still lingered in memory.

Minato bowed his head, uncertain whether the lantern had burned too quickly or exactly as it was meant to.

Reflection

Do you measure your life by its length or by its brightness?

How do you balance sustainability with commitment in each moment?

––––––––

A Moment of Zen

Light a candle and watch it burn. Observe how it flickers and fades.

Reflect on a time when you gave everything to something. How did it feel?

Stand in darkness for a moment. Notice what remains even after the light is gone.

13

THE MONK'S LAST FOOTSTEP

THE WIND ERASED THEIR FOOTPRINTS
as soon as they were made. Akio walked on, un-

hurried, as the younger monks behind him whispered of omens. Akio had taught them many things, but today, he simply walked.

The path twisted through a frozen meadow, each step pressing into the thin layer of snow, leaving behind a fleeting imprint. The younger monks watched the footprints form and fade as the wind carried the frost away. They wondered why their master had brought them here without a word.

Halfway through the meadow, Akio stopped. He turned, looking at the path behind him, then slowly lifted his foot and placed it forward. A sudden gust of wind erased all traces of their passage.

One of the younger monks, Haruki, broke the silence. "Master, our footprints—"

Akio nodded. "Yes."

Haruki hesitated. "Then... where have we been?"

Akio smiled, his breath visible in the cold air. "Where are we now?"

The wind carried his words away before they could settle, and the monks stood in silence, watching as the last trace of their steps disappeared into the white expanse.

Reflection

What remains of the steps you have taken in life?

How do you embrace the present moment when the past fades so quickly?

———

A Moment of Zen

Walk outside on a soft surface and observe your footprints. Watch how they fade.

Stand still and feel the wind on your skin. Imagine it carrying away your worries.

Reflect on something you once clung to that has since vanished. What has taken its place?

14

NO WATER, NO MOON

IN A SECLUDED VALLEY, A NUN NAMED
Chiyo carried a bucket of water up the worn

stone steps of her monastery. The night was cool, and the moon hung low, casting its reflection upon the bucket's surface.

As she neared the entrance, her foot caught on a loose stone. The bucket wobbled, then tumbled from her hands. Water splashed across the ground, vanishing into the dirt. Chiyo stood motionless, watching as the moon's reflection shattered and disappeared.

She let out a slow breath and turned to see her teacher, an elderly nun, watching from the temple's doorway.

"The moon is gone," Chiyo murmured.

Her teacher smiled gently. "Was it ever there?"

Chiyo looked up. The moon remained in the sky, untouched by the spill. A breeze rustled the trees, and she let out a quiet laugh, bowing deeply before stepping inside.

Reflection

**What illusions in your life have felt real,
only to dissolve in an instant?**

**How do you distinguish between what is
fleeting and what is truly lasting?**

———

A Moment of Zen

Fill a bowl with water and watch the
reflections shift as you move.

Drop a small stone into still water and
observe the ripples.

The next time something feels lost, pause—
was it ever truly gone?

15

HOSHIN'S LAST POEM

MASTER HOSHIN HAD LIVED MANY
years, teaching in a small monastery nestled be-

tween the sea and the mountains. One evening, he gathered his students in the courtyard.

"I will leave this world soon," he said.

The younger monks gasped, but the elder ones only nodded. Hoshin had always spoken of impermanence as the way of things.

One student, Renji, bowed deeply. "Master," he asked, "do you know when?"

Hoshin smiled. "Tomorrow, at sunset."

The students murmured among themselves, but none could find words to refute him. The next day, they gathered early, preparing a quiet vigil. The sun dipped lower, casting golden light over the monastery. Hoshin sat calmly in the garden, brush in hand, and wrote his final poem:

> *A fleeting cloud—*
> *The autumn wind takes it far,*
> *Yet the sky remains.*

With a final breath, he set the brush down and closed his eyes. The wind stirred his robes. The sky stretched vast and unbroken.

The students sat in silence. One of them whispered, "Did he leave?"

Another student replied without words, slowly gazing up at the sky.

They all looked up, then.

Reflection

How do you view the impermanence of your own life?

What traces remain of those who have passed before us?

———

A Moment of Zen

Write a short poem about impermanence.
Let it be simple and true.

Watch the sky and observe how clouds come
and go. Notice what stays.

Sit in stillness and reflect on something that
has ended in your life. What remains?

PART IV
Appreciation For the Ordinary

To the mind that is still, the whole universe surrenders.

Chuang Tzu

16

———

EVERYTHING IS BEST

IN A BUSTLING VILLAGE NESTLED ALONG
the rugged coastline, there was a humble shop

where an old fishmonger named Taro had sold his catch for decades.

Each morning, villagers gathered as he arranged the fish upon his wooden stall, their silver scales gleaming in the sun. No matter what the day's catch brought—large or small, common or rare—Taro always placed them down with the same words: "This one is the best."

One busy afternoon, as the sun hung high in the sky, a skeptical traveler passing through the village stopped at the stall. He had heard of Taro's peculiar habit and decided to test him. "Old man," the traveler said, picking up a small fish, "surely this is not the best. Look at this one here—it is much bigger, much fresher."

Taro wiped his hands on his apron and smiled. "That one is the best."

The traveler frowned and pointed to another. "Then what about this fish?"

"That one is also the best."

Frustrated, the traveler crossed his arms. "How can they all be the best?"

Taro simply continued arranging his stall, his hands moving with practiced ease. "If I rejected one, I would be waiting forever for something better." He gestured to the ocean beyond the village. "The sea does not judge what it gives, nor does it wait for the perfect wave."

The traveler stared at the rows of fish, then at Taro, and finally at the endless sea. He stayed silent. Taking a deep breath, he bought the small fish he had first held, feeling its weight in his hands.

The waves continued to roll onto the shore, neither better nor worse than the ones before them.

Reflection

How often do you delay contentment by searching for something better?

What shifts when you accept each moment as it comes?

———

A Moment of Zen

Pick up an ordinary object and say, "This is the best." Notice how your mind reacts.

The next time you eat a meal, appreciate it fully without comparing it to others.

Spend a few minutes watching waves, clouds, or passing people. See if you can let go of judgment.

17

A MOMENT OF TEA

A RESTLESS FISHERMAN ARRIVED AT A weathered fishing dock after many days on the road. The house stood alone at the bend of a quiet river, its wooden walls shaking softly with the wind. Inside, an old woman tended the fire, heating water in an iron kettle.

The traveler sat at the low table, stretching his tired limbs. "I have crossed many mountains and rivers," he sighed. "I have seen great temples and vast cities. But still, I have not found what I seek."

The old woman poured tea into a small cup and placed it before him. "Drink," she said.

The traveler lifted the cup, but before taking a sip, he peered into the liquid. "What kind of tea is this?" he asked.

The old woman stirred the fire. "It is just tea."

The traveler took a hesitant sip. The warmth spread through him, soothing his aching body. He took another sip, then another, feeling the quiet settle around him.

Outside, the river continued its slow journey. The wind rustled the leaves. The fire crackled. The tea was neither rare nor special, yet somehow, it was the most satisfying he had ever tasted.

The traveler looked up, as if about to speak, yet he only exhaled, watching the tide roll in. He set the empty cup down and bowed his head.

The old woman nodded. "Would you like more?"

The traveler smiled. "Yes."

Reflection

**How often do you overlook the simple
moments in search of something greater?**

**What happens when you stop questioning
and
simply experience what is in front of you?**

———

A Moment of Zen

Make a cup of tea and drink it slowly,
focusing on nothing else.

Sit quietly and listen to the sounds around
you without naming them.

Choose something ordinary—a meal, a walk,
a conversation—and be fully present with it.

18

———

THE MAN WHO WALKED WITHOUT FEET

THERE ONCE LIVED AN OLD MAN NAMED
Genzo who had no feet. Yet each day, he moved

through the village with ease, tending his small garden, visiting the river, and sitting beneath the great camphor tree in the village square.

One sunny afternoon, a young boy named Koji watched Genzo make his way along the dirt path. "Elder," Koji asked, running up beside him, "how do you walk with no feet?"

Genzo stopped and looked at the boy. "How do you move when you dream?"

Koji blinked. "I just move."

Genzo nodded and continued down the path. Koji watched him go, his questions unanswered, yet something within him stirred.

The next day, Koji found Genzo near the river, watching the water flow over the rocks. He sat beside him in silence. After a while, Koji spoke. "But in dreams, I do not walk—I simply arrive."

Genzo smiled. "Then tell me, boy, are you dreaming now?"

Koji looked down at his hands, the solid earth beneath him, the sound of the river filling his ears. The question stayed with him long after

Genzo had gone and the mist had lifted from the fields.

Reflection

What limits exist only in your mind, not in reality?

How do you know whether you are moving—or simply being carried?

———

A Moment of Zen

Close your eyes and imagine walking through a familiar place. Notice how effortless it is.

Walk slowly today, paying attention to the feeling of movement itself.

Sit still and listen. Is stillness truly still, or is there always motion within it?

19

THE THREAD THAT WOVE THE WORLD

IN A SMALL SHOP HIDDEN AMONG THE
hills, there lived an elderly weaver named

Naoki. Each day, he sat at his loom, weaving cloth so fine that the villagers swore it held the breath of the wind within its fibers.

One morning, a young woman named Hana approached him, holding a torn piece of fabric. "Master Naoki," she said, "I have heard of your skill. My mother's robe has torn, and I wish to repair it. But when I look at the threads, I cannot see where one begins and another ends."

Naoki took the fabric gently, running his fingers over the weave. "That is because they do not begin or end," he said. "They only continue."

Hana frowned. "But how can that be? This thread must come from somewhere."

Naoki smiled and gestured toward his loom. "Come, watch."

She sat beside him as he worked, her eyes following the shuttle as it passed back and forth. The threads moved as one, crossing, bending, vanishing into the whole.

After a while, Naoki lifted a single thread between his fingers. "Tell me, where does this thread begin?"

Hana traced it with her eyes, but before she could answer, Naoki let it slip back into the cloth, disappearing into the pattern once more.

Outside, the wind passed through the trees, unseen but weaving through every leaf, every blade of grass, every strand of her mother's robe.

She no longer needed an answer.

Reflection

Where in your life do you search for a beginning and an end, when all things may be connected?

How does seeing the whole instead of the parts change your perspective?

———

A Moment of Zen

Run your fingers over a piece of fabric. Notice how each thread disappears into the whole.

Observe the movement of the wind. Though invisible, how does it weave through the world?

Reflect on a relationship or experience. Can you see where it truly began or where it truly ended?

20

A DROP OF WATER

HOW MUCH IS A SINGLE DROP OF WATER
worth?

Tetsuo watched as one fell from the bucket, vanishing into the stone path before him. Each morning, he fetched water from the spring below, filling the temple's cistern drop by drop before walking up a steep hill.

One afternoon, as Tetsuo reached the top, a single drop slipped from the bucket and landed on the dry stone. He paused, watching as it was swallowed by the earth.

The old abbot, seated nearby, observed this and spoke. "Why do you stop?"

Tetsuo furrowed his brow. "I worked hard for this water, and yet, it is gone in an instant."

The abbot nodded. "And do you grieve every breath that leaves your lips?"

Tetsuo blinked, looking down at the bucket still full in his hands. The wind stirred, and somewhere in the distance, the sound of flowing water echoed from the spring below.

That evening, when he carried the next bucket up the hill, another drop fell. This time, he did not stop walking.

Reflection

What small losses in your life have you held onto, even when more remains?

How do you decide when to mourn and when to move forward?

———

A Moment of Zen

Pour a cup of water and watch how it moves before settling.

Notice each breath as it leaves you, neither clinging to it nor resisting it.

The next time something small slips from your grasp, let it go without hesitation.

21

———

THE REAL MIRACLE

A traveling scholar arrived at a
small monastery, eager to witness the great

89

Master Haruto, whose reputation for wisdom had spread far and wide.

When he found the master, Haruto was tending to his garden, pulling weeds with deliberate care. The scholar bowed deeply. "Master, I have heard of your great enlightenment. Tell me, what miracles have you performed?"

Haruto wiped his hands on his robe and smiled. "I have performed many miracles."

The scholar leaned forward, eager to hear of levitation or the secrets of the universe.

Haruto pointed to the mountain beyond the monastery. "Each morning, the sun rises, warming the earth." He gestured toward the village. "Each evening, the moon glows softly above the rooftops." He placed a hand over his stomach. "When I am hungry, I eat. When I am tired, I sleep."

The scholar frowned. "But these are ordinary things. I asked about miracles."

Haruto chuckled, returning to his garden. "And yet, tell me—what greater miracle is there?"

Reflection

What ordinary moments in your life have you overlooked as miracles?

How does seeking something extraordinary prevent you from seeing what is already here?

———

A Moment of Zen

Eat a meal slowly, noticing every texture and taste.

Watch the sunrise or sunset without distraction.

Notice the movement of nature. Watch how a plant, river, or clouds flow with effortless ease.

Message From The Author

Thank you for taking the time to read *The Flow of Zen*. My hope is that these stories have brought you moments of stillness, clarity, or even a small shift in perspective.

This book is part of a larger journey—to share the wisdom of Zen in a simple, accessible way so that more people can experience its teachings and find peace in their lives. In a world that often feels chaotic, even a single story can be a stepping stone to stillness.

If you found value in this book, I'd really appreciate an honest review. Your feedback helps others discover these teachings.

<u>Scan the QR Code or click here to share your thoughts.</u>

Thank you for being part of this journey.

— *Kai*

References

Kapleau, Philip. *The Three Pillars of Zen: Teaching, Practice, and Enlightenment.* New York: Anchor Books, 1989.

Reps, Paul, and Nyogen Senzaki. *Zen Flesh, Zen Bones: A Collection of Zen and Pre-Zen Writings.* Boston: Tuttle Publishing, 1998.

Shunryu, Suzuki. *Zen Mind, Beginner's Mind.* New York: Shambhala Publications, 2006.

Watts, Alan. *The Way of Zen.* New York: Vintage Books, 1957.

Yamada, Koun. *Zen: The Authentic Gate.* Somerville, MA: Wisdom Publications, 2015.

Mark Morse, trans. *The Gateless Gate: The Classic Book of Zen Koans.* Berkeley: Counterpoint, 2019.

Zen Training: Methods and Philosophy. By Katsuki Sekida. Boston: Shambhala Publications, 2005.

www.ingramcontent.com/pod-product-compliance
Lightning Source LLC
Chambersburg PA
CBHW021720190726
48289CB00008B/2625